Magic Wanda's
Travel Emporium

Magic Wanda's Travel Emporium

Tales of Love, Hate and Things in Between

Joshua Searle-White

Skinner House Books
Boston

Printed in the United States

Cover design and text illustrations by Kevin Keane
Text design by Suzanne Morgan
Author photo by Bill Owen

ISBN 1-55896-510-6
978-1-55896-510-2

5 4 3 2 1
08 07 06

Library of Congress Cataloging-in-Publication Data

Searle-White, Joshua.
  Magic Wanda's Travel Emporium : tales of love, hate and things in
between / Joshua Searle-White.
       v. cm.
   Contents: Magic Wanda's Travel Emporium—The storyteller by the
sea—A tale of mismatched love—You just never know—Boing!—In the
boat—Arg and Tharg—Petroleum Pete the Pirate (and the race with
Spectacular Sally)—Enchanted—Adventure calls—Happily ever
after? Yeah, right!—Reduce, re-use, recycle—Sunny Side Mary—One
flower in a field—One world at a time.
   ISBN-13: 978-1-55896-510-2 (pbk. : alk. paper)
   ISBN-10: 1-55896-510-6 (pbk. : alk. paper) 1. Interpersonal
relations--Juvenile fiction. 2. Children's stories, American. [1.
Interpersonal relations--Fiction. 2. Stories.] I. Title.

PZ7.S44127Mag 2006
[Fic]--dc22

2006011562

Contents

Magic Wanda's Travel Emporium

Not too long ago, in a small town not far from here, two young people dreamed of taking a journey together. They sat for hours and talked about the exciting things they would

see—lakes and rivers, mountains and deserts, volcanoes and islands, flowers and fish. They'd heard all about the journeys other people had taken, and they finally decided it was time to experience their own.

So one afternoon they started to pack. At first, it went fine. They got out their backpacks and started collecting all the really important things they might need. There was chocolate, of course (because you can never have too much chocolate), and socks, and flashlights, and rope; and then hiking boots and raincoats and winter hats and water skis; and snowshoes and sunscreen and parachutes and passports and lots and lots of extra underwear. But as they looked at the growing pile, they realized that they had forgotten one thing. They were prepared for anything that might happen—but they didn't have a map. How would they know where they were going?

They went out into their town to look for the right kind of map. They walked for a while, up and down the streets, and finally, down one side street, they caught sight of a sign that looked interesting. It said "Magic Wanda's Travel Emporium— Everything You Need for the Journey of Your Life." All across the front of the store there were pictures—pictures of waterfalls and coral reefs and castles and canals and all kinds of exotic people and animals and amazing food. It looked like just the place, so they pulled open the door and walked in.

It took them a minute to adjust to the darkness inside, and once they did, they found something very strange. Despite the colorful sign and all the pictures out front, inside, the store was completely empty. There were no shelves, no drawers, no tents or snorkels or guidebooks or anything! And most importantly, there were no maps. The only thing in the store was a single bare counter way in the back. Behind the counter sat an old woman, watching them peacefully as they stared at the blank walls.

The two young people looked around.

"There's nothing here," said the first one. "Let's go."

And they were about to leave, but something about the way the old woman looked at them made them turn back.

"Let's at least talk to her," said the second one. "Maybe we can find out why there's nothing here."

So they walked past the bare walls to the counter at the back of the store.

"Hello," one of them said. "We've decided to go on a long journey, and we need some help. We came in because your sign says you have everything for the journey of your life, but there's nothing here at all! We're leaving tomorrow, Monday, so we need to get ready very quickly. Can you help us?"

"Ah, yes," said Magic Wanda (because that was who the old woman was, of course) in a high, thin voice. "You're leaving on a great journey on Tuesday, and you need advice."

"No, Monday is when we are leaving," came the answer. "*Monday*. And that's why . . ."

"And then you are leaving for a great journey on Wednesday," Wanda continued. "I'm beginning to understand."

The young people looked at each other. "No," said the other one, "I don't think you understand at all. It's *tomorrow*,

Monday, that we are leaving. That's why we're here to get some help!"

"Yes, of course, of course." said Wanda. "You are leaving Monday. But on a journey like this, you don't just leave once and then be done with it. Oh, no. No, on this kind of journey, every day you set off all over again. Every day you get up and decide: Am I going on this journey, with my traveling companion, or am I staying here? And then, if you are ready for adventure, only then do you set off once again. So yes, you are leaving tomorrow. And you are leaving Tuesday. *And* you are leaving Wednesday. And every day after that, and every day after that."

The young people looked at each other and nodded. "Okay, then," said one. "But we still have a problem. Even though we have lots of stuff we can take, we don't have what we really need: a map to tell us where to go. Do you have one?"

"Ah, yes, a map." said Wanda. "A map to tell you which direction you should go. Well, you know, there's a funny thing about maps. You have to be careful of them. You see, a map is someone's idea of what the world looks like. It's not the actual world. Do you know that some people make maps of places where they have never actually been? And other people make maps of places like rain forests and flower gardens that change from day to day, so a map made last week won't help you today. And sometimes the route one person would take is completely the wrong route for someone else. There is no one way that works for everyone, and no one has ever taken the exact journey you're going to take. So get a bunch of maps and read them, but then make your own decisions about where to go."

The young people thought for a minute, and then one replied, "I suppose you could be right. But there are so many things we want to see. Shouldn't we have a map that tells us where all the most interesting things are?"

"Yes, oh, yes!" Wanda answered. "There are lots of interesting things in the world. But some of the most interesting and exciting things won't show up on any map at all. Let's say that you are walking in a very narrow gorge, with steep cliffs rising on each side, and suddenly you come across a rock blocking your path. It's a huge rock, and there doesn't seem to be any way around it. You could sit there for years, thinking that it is nothing but a rock. And yet, there might be all kinds of interesting things that you could learn about the rock. How did it get there? What does it feel like if you lay your cheek on it? Is it hot or cold? If you put your back to it and push, does it move? What if you sit in front of it and sing to it? You never know what might happen. You see, even a rock blocking your path has a story. You can always find something new and exciting to learn—if you look for it. Everything is an adventure."

"Well, okay," said the other. "Maybe that's true. But what if a storm comes up, or we get chased by tigers or something. Shouldn't we have a map that tells us where the safe places are so we can run and hide if we need to?"

"I suppose so," Wanda answered. "If you're being chased by tigers or a storm comes up that's so strong it could blow you off a mountain—well, then, I would recommend taking shelter. But be careful. The thing about safe, comfortable places is that they are fun to enjoy for a while, but you can get kind of used to them. Some people even find a safe, beautiful place, like a warm cave, and they think that their journey is over. But it's not like that. Warm caves are great, but if you run to them whenever some danger threatens . . . well, then, you'll never know the joy of standing in the wind, and feeling the pelting of the rain, and hearing the rumbling of the thunder. And most importantly, if you stay in the safe places, you'll never find out what is behind the next hill. So, sure, find the safest and most beautiful places, and see what they are like. And *then* go see what adventures you can find."

"Well, if all this is true," the young people said, "is there anything you think we absolutely need for our journey?"

"Oh, yes, yes, yes!" said Wanda. "Of course! There is one thing that people always forget on this kind of journey, and it's really important."

She reached under the counter and brought out some paper and a pen. "You see, people often leave on this kind of journey, and they figure they should do it totally on their own. But it doesn't work that way. Yes, the path you take is up to the two of you, but you can't do it alone. No journey is complete without company, and no matter how much fun your traveling companion is, you need to let others be a part of your journey too. Talk to people, help them though their difficult mountain passes, and let them help you through yours. We're all on our own journeys, after all."

Magic Wanda paused and looked at the couple. "Take the paper and pen as my present," she said. "Write letters. Keep in touch." Then she stood up. "I think you are ready for your trip. Don't you?"

The young people looked at Wanda and then back at each other. "I guess we are," one said, as the other took the paper and pen from Wanda's hand. "Thank you."

"Happy travels," said Wanda, and the young people walked out of the store, and down the street, and back to where they were packing to leave.

And the very next day, with their pen and paper and just a few necessary things, they set off on their journey. The next day after that they set off again, and the next day after that, *and* the next day after that.

Through storms and mountains, tigers and crystal-sand beaches, through every kind of beauty and every kind of challenge, every day was a new adventure. And as far as anyone knows, the young people are still out there somewhere, together on their journey.

A Tale of Mismatched Love

Woodrow was a clarinet, and he was gorgeous as only a clarinet could be. He was tall, straight, and black, with shining silver keys. He had a beautiful clarinet voice and could sing notes that were way up high and notes that were way down low, all with softness and ease. He was very polite and well mannered. Some people called him stiff and formal, and to tell the truth, he was kind of rigid . . . but after all, he was a clarinet, and that's what clarinets are like.

Woodrow liked being a clarinet, doing the things that clarinets do, singing music with his clarinet friends. But he had one major problem. He was in love with a saxophone. Her name was Alta, and Woodrow liked everything about her. She was golden and shiny, with a big round bell. She was curvy from top to bottom, not straight like Woodrow, and when she sang, she was jazzy and relaxed. Woodrow thought she was fantastic, and in fact, she was. He was so in love with her that he even made up a song about it. It went like this:

"I'm in love . . . with . . . a saxophone.
I'm in love with a saxophone.
We go together like a dog and a bone.
I'm in love with a saxophone."

All Woodrow wanted was to be with Alta. He thought about her night and day. The problem was that he knew he was very different from her. He was really straight, and she was so curvy and jazzy. He figured that she would never like him as he was, so he decided to see if he could get looser. He even changed his song to make it more cool:

"I'm in love (ooh-ahh!) with a saxophone.
I'm in love (chikky-boom!) with a saxophone.
We go together (yeah, yeah!) like a dog and a bone.
I'm in love (cool, man!) with a saxophone."

There were other problems too. For one thing, where Woodrow and Alta live, clarinets and saxophones don't really mix that much. Clarinets mostly play in orchestras and saxophones play in jazz bands. They don't live in the same neighborhoods or go to the same parties. Plus, Woodrow's family didn't think that being in love with a saxophone was a very good idea. His older sister said, "A saxophone? A saxophone? Come on, Woodrow, get real. Saxophones are not like us. They may have reeds, but that's the end of it. They're a different color. They're made of different stuff. They're . . . so . . . so shiny, and brassy, and . . . and horny! They're twisted! They're out of control. You're making a big mistake; stay away from them!"

But, of course, Woodrow couldn't. Every time he thought of Alta, he felt so happy and so in love. So one day he decided to try talking to her. He was nervous, of course.

"What if she doesn't like me? Am I cool enough? Am I relaxed enough? Am I hip enough?" But he went over to her side of town and to her house, and he knocked on the door, and she opened it.

"Woodrow! What a surprise! What brings you here?" said Alta.

"Well, I, uh, I, uh, oh, yeah . . . ," Woodrow said, desperately trying to be cool.

"Are you all right?" asked Alta. "You're acting kind of strange!"

"Oh, ahh, oh . . . yeah. I just wanted to see if you would like to go for a walk," stammered Woodrow.

"A walk? Well . . . sure, why not?" she said.

And so they went walking. Woodrow was excited. "This is great!" he thought to himself. "I can see it all now—a wedding, a nice home, a family." Then he realized he wasn't saying anything, so he tried to think of something to talk about. "So, Alta," he said, "listen to any good music lately?"

"Well, sure," she answered. "I heard a great jazz piece just last night!"

"Jazz?" said Woodrow. "What about, um, Mozart?"

"Well," Alta sighed, "he never wrote music for saxophone, so I don't listen to him too much."

"Oh, no!" Woodrow said to himself. "This isn't going well at all!" Then he said out loud, "Oh, right. Well, play in any good orchestras lately?"

Alta looked at him strangely. "Woodrow, you know that orchestras hardly ever let saxophones play in them. What are you thinking?"

"This is getting worse and worse!" he thought. "What do I do next? Oh, wait, I know," and said, "Hey, aren't trumpets and trombones obnoxious?"

"Well, that's for sure!" Alta answered.

Woodrow felt a little better now. They continued walking a bit, and then Woodrow said, "Hey, Alta, look at that hill over there. Do you know that it's my absolute favorite place in the world?"

"Really? Why?"

"Well, if you stand up on that hill, the sun sets right over the town down there. I like to come up here in the late afternoon, sing a few quiet notes, and then stand here, very still. It turns out that if you stand very still for a long time, you can actually see the sun disappear behind the buildings. Hey, it's just about the right time! Let's do it; let's stand right here and watch!"

"Um, wait a minute," said Alta. "Are you saying that you like to stand here, not moving? Just stand here? And watch the sun go down?"

"Sure!" laughed Woodrow. "Just try it. You'll like it!"

Alta looked at him sadly. "Um, Woodrow, I'm not sure how to break this to you, but I don't like standing around. I like to move, to sway, to dance, to swing! I don't like to just be still."

"Can't you just try it, Alta? You might think it's really great!"

"Woodrow, look at me. Let's get real for a minute. You and I are similar in some ways, but we are very different in others. Okay, we've both got reeds. Okay, we've both got keys. But when it comes to standing and looking at sunsets . . . well, you are built for standing. You're flat at the bottom, and you can stand up like a glass or a vase does. But not me. I'm curved. I can't just stand still or I'll fall over. I need to be moving. That's who I am, and I can't be anything else."

Woodrow was heartbroken. She was right. He was built for standing, and she was built for movement. There was no way she could stand and watch the sunset. They really were very different, after all. Too different.

They walked back to her house. Alta said goodbye and went inside.

All the way home, Woodrow talked to himself. "What a disaster! I can't believe I did that. Falling in love with a saxophone—what was I thinking? It could never work. Saxophones are too different, too loose, too unstable. From now on, it's clarinets for me, and that's all!"

But he realized that if he went home right now, he'd have to listen to his sister saying, "I told you so!" He thought he'd go up to the hill instead, play a few notes, and watch the sunset. That might make him feel better.

As he got close, he realized that somebody was already up there. He walked a bit closer and saw that it was . . . well, he wasn't sure what it was. She was gold and shiny like a saxophone, but straight and flat at the bottom like a clarinet. He walked up to her and said, "What are you doing here?"

And she answered, "Not much. I just like this place. I like to come up here in the late afternoon, and sing a few quiet notes, and then stand here, very still, and watch the sun go down. Did you know that if you stand very, very still, for a long time, you can actually see the sun disappear behind the buildings?"

Woodrow was amazed. "What?" he said. "I, uh . . . I mean, yes, actually, I knew that, because I come up here pretty often. But wait a minute. Who are you? What are you? Are you a saxophone?"

"Yes, of course," she said.

"How can you be a saxophone? You're straight, like me, and saxophones are curved. They don't like to stand still, to watch sunsets and stuff. No way can you be a saxophone! You must be something else!"

"Well," she replied, laughing, "just because I'm a saxophone doesn't mean we're all the same! Soprano saxophones like me are straight, and others, like tenors and baritones, are curved. Some like to stand and watch sunsets, while others would rather dance and move all the time. We're all different. You know, you should be careful about thinking that you know what someone's like before you even talk to them! Oh, look, the sun is just starting to go behind that hill. Let's stand very quietly, and I'll sing a few notes, and we'll watch it go down."

Woodrow was speechless, which was a good thing, because at that moment she began to sing a few quiet notes. The beauty of her voice took Woodrow's breath away. It was high and sweet but at the same time rich and beautiful. He had never heard anything like it. When she finished, he simply stood in awe.

A few minutes later she spoke. "Isn't that sunset amazing?"

And Woodrow answered, "It sure is. It's beautiful. By the way, what's your name?"

"Penny. What's yours?"

"Woodrow," he said, still struck by the beauty of the sunset, the music, and the moment.

"Well," said Penny, "I'm pleased to meet you, Woodrow. Maybe I'll see you up here again tomorrow?"

"Um, yeah," Woodrow managed to say. "I mean, yes, I'll definitely be here!"

Woodrow came back the next day, and Penny was there. And the next day, and the next, and the next. They got to be closer and closer friends the longer they knew each other. Of course, it wasn't easy; inter-instrumental relationships never are. But the ways they were similar and the ways they were different made the music they created together beautiful, and interesting, and romantic, and exciting, all at the same time.

Sometimes love is not as mismatched as you might think.

You Just Never Know

Tessa and Murray had been married for years
Since the days of their long-ago youth.
And their living together, while happy and smooth,
Was kind of boring, to tell you the truth.

See, Tessa and Murray knew each other so well
They could predict what each other would do.
What they'd feel, what they'd want, what they'd say,
    what they'd think,
There was nothing unexpected or new.

Long ago they had started a schedule
Of what they would eat on each day.
The menu never altered, the plan never faltered
For years it had gone on that way.

So: cheese sticks on Mondays, and eggplant on Tuesdays,
On Wednesdays, raisins for lunch.
Raw tofu on Thursdays, baked beans on Fridays,
And pickles for Saturday brunch.

Now how'd they decide on that strange group of foods?
Did they look for the ones that were cheap?
Did they test them and try them, boil them and fry them
Then figure out which ones to keep?

Well, no. They didn't. They never really talked
About what foods to put in their pot
Because they could just tell by seeing the signals
What the other would like and would not.

If Murray ate something that he didn't like
His nostrils would show a small strain
And when Tessa saw that, she knew right away
That dinner should go down the drain!

And Tessa had just the same kind of small signs.
For Murray, she was never a mystery.
If he brought home a bagel, and Tessa said, "Hmm . . ."
Then he knew that bagel was history.

And so it went on, day after day
After month after month after year
Pickles and cheese sticks and baked beans and eggplant.
No spaghetti, no cheesecake, no beer!

But you know, all this time, though she never did show it
Tessa was getting so bored
That she thought "One more raisin or chunk of raw tofu
And I think I'll go out of my gourd!"

But she was so sure Murray liked all that stuff
And though it was really absurd
She wanted him to be happy and pleased
So she ate it, without even a word.

But it finally happened, one day in late summer,
Though she knew it would start a big fight.
Over a plate of fried eggplant and raisins and pickles
She screamed, "I just can't take one more bite!"

And then she thought, "Now I've done it.
He'll be mad and upset, he'll be furious.
I've gone against everything Murray believes!"
But Murray said something quite curious.

"I am so glad you said that, Tessa my sweet.
I would never want to make you uneasy
But the eggplant and raisins are driving me crazy
And the pickles are making me queasy!"

She said, "What? You don't want all that stuff?"
He said, "I eat it 'cause I thought that you do!
I've kept my mouth shut so as not to upset you."
Then Tessa said, "I thought that I knew you!"

And so Murray started telling Tessa some things
That made her go white with amazement.
He said that he really liked blue cheese and pretzels
And had been sneaking them down in the basement!

And there was more too, like pancakes and tacos
That Murray'd been wanting and craving.
He had also been dying to eat a big sundae
With chocolate ice cream he'd been saving.

Tessa felt strange to have all of this happen
To have Murray be so unconventional.
Could he really be different than she'd always thought?
And not nearly so . . . one-dimensional?

And as they talked on, Tessa found it was true.
Murray had such food creativity
And Tessa began to find that she too
Had untapped culinary progressivity!

And after they talked and wondered and laughed
Their worries had never been fewer.
They took all the raisins and baked beans and pickles
And tossed them right into the sewer.

From that day on they were more devoted than ever
And their marriage had never been greater.
They had love and adventure and wonder and happiness
And a complex and full 'frigerator.

And that's how they learned that no matter their age
Or how long they had both been together,
They weren't so easy to know and predict;
They were as changeable and wild as the weather.

Tessa and Murray had found deep new feelings
As complex as snowflakes in snow.
And the moral? You've probably figured it out.
The fact is, you just never know.

Boing!

This is a story about a planet pretty much like the one we live on, with trees, and sun, and houses, and everything else, except for one thing: the people on it look like red, round, rubber balls. Of course, the kids are smaller than the grown-ups, and some are slightly different shades of red than others. But overall, they look like red, round, rubber balls.

Now, even though these people have houses and families and jobs and cars, just like we do, being red rubber balls makes them a little bit different from us. For example, when they roll out of bed in the morning, they *really* roll out of bed. And when parents complain that their kids are bouncing off the walls, they really are bouncing off the walls. (You can imagine how much fun that would be!) But the biggest difference from us is in the way they act with their friends.

Take the Red Rubber Ball Elementary School. If you looked at the playground during recess, you'd see all the kids out playing together. And for them, that means that they'd be bouncing off each other. Boing! One would roll really fast towards a friend, and boing! they'd bump into each other and bounce off in different directions. Then they'd roll back towards each other, and boing! bounce off in another direction. Sometimes several of them would come together at the same time. Boingboingboing! They'd really fly in different directions. Sometimes they would aim at each other but miss entirely. Whoosh! They'd roll past each other to opposite ends of the playground.

They could actually be in the same place for only a moment before one or both or all would go flying—if they were ever together at all. Now this was okay a lot of the time, but sometimes it wasn't.

Like one day there was this girl named Helen who had a secret that she wanted to tell her best friend, Sally. It was a great secret, a juicy, interesting secret that only Helen knew. It was so great that Helen had been looking forward to telling Sally ever since she first rolled out of bed that morning.

So as soon as Helen got to school, she went looking for Sally, and after a few minutes, found her on the playground. There were kids everywhere, rolling and bouncing and boinging and whooshing so fast that Helen could hardly hear her own voice as she called to Sally. Sally was bouncing all over the place too, and it was really hard to get her attention.

Finally, Helen managed to get them both into a quiet part of the playground. She rolled over to Sally and tried to tell her about the secret: "Sally, I've got this . . ." Boing! Off she rolled and then rolled back, ". . . secret that . . ." Boing! Rolling off and then back again, ". . . you've got to hear . . ." Boing! "I need to tell you . . ." Whoosh!

It was impossible! After all, secrets aren't the kind of thing you can just shout out on a playground filled with kids. But every time Helen got close enough to tell Sally the secret, boing!, she'd go flying off again. Helen began to get very frustrated. Then the bell rang, and they had to go in to class.

As the day went on, Helen tried and tried to tell Sally the secret. At lunch she saw Sally going off to the bathroom and followed her. She thought that maybe in a small room they'd be able to talk. It turned out to be even worse than on the playground. Instead of big bounces, she ended up making lots of little bounces from Sally to the bathroom walls and back:

"Sal (boing boing) ly (boing) I've (boing) got (boing boing) this (boing boing) secret (boing) to (boingboingboing) . . ." That idea didn't work at all. Helen was getting seasick!

During afternoon recess, Helen tried something else. She rolled up and bumped Sally into a corner, thinking Sally would stay still while Helen talked. She pushed up against Sally, saying as fast as she could, "I've got this secret I'm going to tell you. Listen it's really great . . . ," but finally, so much pressure built up that BOING! Helen bounced off again, this time even further than usual.

Next Helen tried bouncing way up into the air and coming down and landing on Sally. But boooiiinnnggg, back up into the air Helen went!

It was really frustrating. The whole day Helen tried to tell Sally the secret, but she could never be with her for more than a few seconds at a time.

Finally, it was time to go home. Most of the kids had already gone, and Helen and Sally were rolling down the hallway towards the exit. Once more, Helen tried to get close to Sally, but as usual, she kept bouncing off her. Boing, off Sally, boing, off the wall, boing, off Sally, boing, off the wall.

Helen got so upset and tired that she just stopped trying. She rolled into the center of the hall and just rocked there, leaning slightly over to her left side. Suddenly, Sally had an idea. She rolled to a stop next to Helen and leaned just slightly towards her right, and they met.

When Helen looked up, there was Sally, leaning ever so lightly against her, both of them barely moving. She could hear Sally breathing. She could almost hear her own heart beating. Best of all, she realized, she could tell Sally anything she wanted and talk as long as she wanted, and nothing would stop her. And it was so easy!

Filled with this exciting new feeling, Helen looked at Sally and started to tell her the secret. "You're not going to believe this. Yesterday, when I got home after school . . . ."

Well, we'll let Helen and Sally keep their secret a secret. But if *you* ever want to tell your friend a secret without bouncing off them, now you know how. Not with a boing or a whoosh, but with just a simple lean.

In the Boat

Let me tell you all a story
About two people in a boat.
It was old, and it was rickety
And it could barely float.

The boat was bobbin'
On the deep blue sea
And the boy said to the girl
"Come sit next to me!"

The girl said to the boy
"Not a chance of that!
Last time I was over there
You almost knocked me flat!

You said you were just playin'
As you tossed around that ball,
But I did not like it
Not very much at all.

It made me very mad
As I think that you'll agree,
So if you want some company
You come next to me!"

Well, that boat kept floatin'
They were quiet as could be
And that boat kept on bobbin'
On the deep blue sea.

So, they sat and they sat
And nothing did improve
And the girl said to the boy
"You gonna make your move?"

And the boy said to the girl,
"Well, I'll tell you what I think.
The last time I came over there
You almost knocked me in the drink!

"Y'know, down there in the water
There's fishies from the reef.
Sharks and barracudas
Lots of stuff with scary teeth!

"But you didn't care, no
You wanted to be cool
And jump up and down
Breakin' every boatin' rule.

"And you rocked this boat
From the bottom to the top
And you woulda knocked us both in
If I hadn't said to stop!

"So if you wanna
Be sittin' knee to knee,
It's all up to you, girl.
You come here to me."

31

And the boat kept floatin'
They were quiet as could be
And the boat kept bobbin'
On the deep blue sea.

So they sat.
And they sat.
Angry eyes.
What a spat!

"You come to me!"
"No, you come to me!"
"It's all your fault!"
"You're as wrong as you could be!"

Well, I just have to tell you
It was not a pretty sight,
The two of them just sittin' there
Spoilin' for a fight.

It was days, maybe weeks
They were sittin' in the cold.
It was dull and it was boring.
It was gettin' pretty old.

So the girl said to herself
"Now this is pretty dumb.
I'm hungry and I'm thirsty
And my toes are getting numb!

"So maybe I should go and sit
With jerkface anyway.
It's better than just freezing here
another blasted day."

So the girl jumped up and said
"All right, okay, I'll go!"
But there was something that the girl
Didn't kinda know.

The boy had been thinkin' too
About what fools they were.
He jumped up, and as she moved
He crashed right into her!

And they both went woozy.
The collision was a doozie.
They both yelled, "Aieee!"
And they fell into the sea.

Well as they fell into the sea
They thought that they were dead,
But something else was going on
That felt real good instead.

It turned out they were swimmers
They flipped and dove like fish!
It was like they were dancing
With a turn and with a swish.

The boat was soon forgotten
As they swam and danced and played
And farther and farther
From the boat they strayed.

And deeper still and farther still
Past reefs and rocks they darted.
They didn't need the boat at all
Since something new had started.

Where they are now, I couldn't say
'Cause it's a big wide sea.
But I can say they'll stay out there,
Alive, and happy, and free.

(Tap your foot slowly to keep the rhythm of this story.
Pause for a few beats between stanzas.)

Arg and Tharg

In a wet and cold streambed, underneath a big bridge, lived a troll named Arg. Now, in case you don't remember about trolls, let's do a bit of review. What are trolls like? Well, they are smelly and dirty, and they love to lounge in muddy, disgusting

water under bridges. It's even better if the water is cold. And they eat gross, repulsive things, like worm fricassee and snail sauce and snake-bladder stew. And, of course, they're irritable. You would be too, if you ate that kind of stuff every day.

And what do trolls do? They sit in their streambeds, waiting until fat goats come trip-trip-tripping along over the bridge. Then they climb up onto the bridge, grab the goats, and eat them up. Or at least they try to.

One day, Arg was down in the streambed, sipping on some ant juice, when he heard the sound of hooves trip-trip-tripping over the bridge. It sounded like a nice, fat goat, a much better dinner than what was available down in the stream.

So he climbed up along the side of the bridge and stuck up his big old head to look. He was about to growl in his gravelly troll voice, "Arr, who's that trip-trip-tripping over my bridge?" when he heard another troll voice, a higher and squeakier one, saying, "Ha-ha! Who's that trip-trip-tripping across my bridge?"

Arg was startled. He looked across to the other side of the bridge, and sure enough, there was another troll head sticking up! This troll, whose name was Tharg, was a bit smaller than Arg but every bit as dirty, smelly, and loud. What was she doing here?

Arg was not happy. "Hey! I troll of bridge!" he shouted. "This my bridge! Go away."

"What?" shrieked Tharg. "No way. I troll of bridge! I catch goat and eat for supper!"

"You catch goat? Hah! You too weak and small. I catch goat!" said Arg.

"No way!" Tharg said. "You too out of shape. You never catch goat. Goat mine!" And with that, she started to climb up onto the top of the bridge to get the goat.

But as she did, Arg swung down under the bridge. He stuck out his big foot and pushed her right off the side of the bridge down, down, down into the stream, where she landed with a big splash. He hung off the side of the bridge, sticking out his tongue at Tharg, taunting her and making rude noises. Then he climbed up to get the goat—but the goat was long gone, eating the nice green grass on the other side. And laughing at the trolls, too.

Tharg was mad. Really mad. She pulled herself out of the stream, screaming the whole time. "You bad troll! You knock me off bridge! That very unfair. I get you for that!"

Tharg started to climb up the bank. As she did, another goat came trip-trip-tripping over the bridge.

Once more, Arg stuck his big head over the side of the bridge and was about to say, "Who's that trip-trip-tripping over my bridge?" but Tharg sneaked right up and pulled on his suspenders (trolls always wear suspenders), and Arg went falling down, down, down. He splashed into the stream. And Tharg hung there, thumbing her nose at him while he sputtered in the water. The goat, of course, went trip-trip-tripping over the bridge, and off to eat some of the nice green grass.

Well, Arg was mad. He got up out of the muck and yelled "Hey! This *my* bridge. You no right to push me in river!"

Tharg answered, "Oh, yeah? I very right. Number one, you started it. Number two, you steal my dinner. Number three, I smarter, faster, and braver than you. And number four, nya-nya-nya, you in water and I on bridge!"

Now, just as she was taunting Arg, a third goat came trip-trip-tripping onto the bridge (which, of course, didn't seem as dangerous now as it used to). Arg started climbing back onto the bridge as fast as his troll feet could carry him. Tharg started to say, "Who's that trip-trip-tripping . . . ," and just as she spoke, Arg threw a rock and whacked her right on the forehead. As Tharg fell, she grabbed Arg's foot, and then she tried to reach up and grab his hair, but she missed and grabbed his nose instead. Arg lost his grip on the bridge, and they both went falling together down, down, down to the stream, fighting the whole way, until they both hit the water with a tremendous splash.

They spluttered up to the top of the water, punching and kicking and screaming at each other.

"I right! You wrong!" yelled Tharg.

"No, I right! You wrong!" yelled Arg.

The more they fought, the more tangled they got. Arg got his fingers stuck in Tharg's hair, and Tharg's big toe got stuck in Arg's nose. Tharg's shirt button got caught in Arg's bootlace, and Arg's suspenders got wrapped around Tharg's elbow.

They finally got themselves to the side of the stream, all tangled together, elbowing each other and kneeing each other and banging into each other and cursing at each other the whole way. They pulled themselves up onto the bank and lay there, totally exhausted and angry.

And the goat, of course, tripped over to the other side of the bridge and began eating the sweet grass there. Now all three goats stood there, laughing at the trolls.

Arg was furious. Tharg was furious. They shouted and screamed at each other and tried to stand up. But they kept getting more and more entangled, and finally, they just stopped.

"This your fault!" screamed Arg.

And Tharg said, "This not my fault! I innocent victim, and you mean and nasty troll!"

"Me mean and nasty? No! You mean and nasty. You evil. I get lawyer and sue your pants off!"

"Oh, yeah? I get lawyer and sue your pants off!"

They started fighting again. And as they kept fighting, they got more and more tangled, with their hair catching on each other's buttons, and their toes getting stuck in each other's noses. It went on like that until way, way late in the afternoon. As the sun set, the goats headed home back over the bridge, laughing all the way.

And still the trolls lay there at the side of the stream.

Now the thing is, at this point, the trolls really had only two choices. They could keep fighting, and get more and more tangled up, and probably die of starvation. Or they could try something different to find a way out.

What did they do? Well, you can go ask them, because they are still lying there on that stream bank, cursing at each other:

"I right! You wrong!"

"No, I right! You wrong!"

You see, they're trolls. They're not too bright. They're mean and nasty. They never forgive, or make up, or do anything new or unusual. But we're people. If we were in this situation, we'd do something different, right?

Petroleum Pete the Pirate

(and the Race with Spectacular Sally)

Petroleum Pete was a picture-perfect pirate. He had a peg leg, a pointy, pimpled nose, pierced ears, and a pudgy potbelly. He was pugnacious, he was profane, and he was proud. He had a pirate ship called the *Pearl of Persia*, and from its prow to its poop deck the Pearl was as pretty as a picture. Pete was particularly proud of the *Pearl of Persia* and wouldn't permit any person to pronounce pejoratives pertaining to her. Pete was a politician, too. He was so powerful and pioneering a pirate that everyone called him "El Primo Piraté," and in return for his patronage, they praised and promoted him in all the proximate provinces.

Yep, Petroleum Pete was pretty pleased with himself. His purse was piled with plenty of pennies, and his *Pearl of Persia* was praised as precious and perfect by all the other pirates. He had plenty of patrons who plied him with peaches and pancakes and Pop-tarts to eat. He had plush places to play and posh pictures in his parlor. Sure, he was pretentious, predictable, and perhaps a bit pompous. But if you put it in perspective, Petroleum Pete was sitting pretty . . . until Spectacular Sally sailed into the city.

Now Spectacular Sally came from Snarkstown, a sleazy city in the South. She sailed in on her sloop, the *Sassy Sister*, with her snappy sidekick, a sinister scorpion named Samantha, at her side. And Spectacular Sally was *something*. She was as strong as Sampson on steroids and stubborn as a steer. She was sneaky as a snake. *And* what's more, she was smart. She could sell a snowball to a Scandinavian or sign up a squid for swimming lessons. Oh, she was a slickster, all right. Sure, she was strident and sanctimonious, and sometimes seriously scatological. But she was sincere. And when she sauntered into the central city square one sunny Saturday, she started a significant stir.

Sally scaled a stone in the center of the city square and shouted, "I'm Spectacular Sally, Scourge of the Seven Seas! No one can sail as swiftly as me and my *Sassy Sister*! I'm the new star of this city! And I'll slay any scalawag who suggests otherwise!"

Well, Petroleum Pete couldn't permit this kind of prattle! "Oh, yeah?" Pete protested. "I'm Petroleum Pete the Pirate, and *I'm* the Primo Piraté around this place. You just plop yourself back in that pile of planks you call a pirate ship and push off back to whatever pathetic puddle you pulled your pug-nosed self out of! The *Pearl of Persia* is the prince of this province!"

"That sad-looking second-rate sack of scum?" shouted Spectacular Sally. "Don't be silly! That scow would sink in a second if it sought to sail swifter than my *Sassy Sister*!"

"Oh, yeah?" pontificated Petroleum Pete. "My *Pearl of Persia* makes that pathetic pothole of yours look like a puddle-plowing pickle!"

"Well, you're nothing but a simpering, slobbering, snot-nose!" yelled Sally.

"And you're just a pint-sized pipsqueak!" roared Pete.

"Sissy!" screamed Sally.

"Punk!" pounded Pete.

"Sourpuss!"

"Pinhead!"

"May I have a moment, may I have a moment," murmured a mustached man in the mob. It was the mayor of the metropolis, a moon-faced man named Mitchell. "You mustn't mistreat each other so mercilessly. All this malicious mocking will mostly make you more mad. May I mention a method to mollify this misunderstanding? A match, a meet, a race. The one who musters the most moxie will merit a medal and be maintained as the most meritorious mariner in our midst!"

"A race!" yelled all the townspeople. "A race! A race!"

Petroleum Pete and Spectacular Sally looked at each other. Pete was peeved. Sally was seething.

"Sure," said Sally.

"I'll participate," said Pete.

And so Spectacular Sally sashayed back to the *Sassy Sister*, while Pete pounded the pier to the *Pearl of Persia*.

"The match will be to Iceberg Island and back," intoned Mayor Mitchell. "Iceberg Island is an itty-bitty but idyllic and isolated island, intermittently inhabited by interested individuals for intimate interludes, but its isolation and insignificance make it ideal for this initiative."

Pete piled into the *Pearl of Persia*, and Sally scampered onto the *Sassy Sister*. At a mention from the mayor, the race was on.

Out into the water they went. The wind whipped the waves, and water washed over the weather-beaten wet wood. At first Petroleum Pete pushed past Spectacular Sally, yelling, "Hah, you pathetic piker! Perceive my poop deck as it plows past!"

But a few minutes later the wind went to the west, and Spectacular Sally surged ahead, yelling, "Ha-ha, you simpering slowpoke! Your sluggish ship stinks like socks!"

On and on they went, hour after hour, first Petroleum Pete passing Sally, then Spectacular Sally surpassing Pete. But as they inched towards Iceberg Island, an incredible incident intervened. A huge wall of water, a behemoth breaker, a stupendous swell surged out of the sea, picked up the *Pearl of Persia* and the *Sassy Sister*, and threw them up into the air and down onto Iceberg Island. Pete plummeted into a puddle. Sally splashed down in the sand. But the *Pearl of Persia* plunged onto a pile of pointed pebbles, and the *Sassy Sister* slammed into some sharpened stones, and each splintered into a pile of shards and pieces.

Sally struggled to sit up. Pete pulled himself out of the puddle. They both looked at the shattered parts of their ships.

"Now what?" pouted Pete. "The *Pearl* is in pieces! She's been pulverized!"

"And the *Sister*!" shouted Sally. "She's been smashed! She's in slivers!"

"You pompous poophead!" yelled Pete. "If it weren't for your protestations of pirate proficiency, the *Pearl* would be in one piece!"

"Oh, stow it, you simpering snotnose," said Sally. "It's your own stupid swaggering that stuck us here!"

"Oh, yeah?" protested Pete.

"Yeah!" said Sally. "Now you just stay silent while I sew up the *Sister* with . . . with strands of seaweed."

"Oh, yeah? Well, I'll patch the *Pearl* with pieces of . . . of . . . palm trees," parroted Pete.

"And the *Sister* will sail so swiftly that she'll . . . uh . . . see the shore before sundown!"

"And the *Pearl* will . . . will peel out and pounce on the pirate property prior to the peak of night!"

"I'll be slurping . . . um . . . snowcones by . . . by seven o'clock!"

"I'll be perching on my . . . uh . . . pillow . . . um, probably."

They looked at each other.

"This is certainly stupid," said Sally.

"Pretty pathetic," said Pete.

"Our ships are in splinters," said Sally. "I don't see a single solution."

"It's pointless," agreed Pete. "These piles of planks are like puzzle pieces that can't be put in place."

"We'll sit here until the next century."

"We'll be perpetual prisoners."

They sat for a moment. Then Sally looked thoughtful.

"Wait," she said. "Wait. What if we . . . salvage some pieces from the *Pearl* and the *Sister*, and see if we can put them together?"

"What?" said Pete. "Me, s . . . s . . . s . . . salvage pieces? Preposterous! There'd be pandemonium!"

"It seems like our only possibility," said Sally.

"You mean," said Pete despairingly, "Pull strong sections that are perfect out of the pile, and stick them together into one pirate sailing ship?"

"Precisely!" said Sally.

"Ohhhh," said Pete. "I'm glad my poor papa can't see me now!"

So Sally and Pete started the preparations. They scoured the pile of pieces and selected the most perfect sizes. Together they patched and sawed, sewed and pounded. By evening they had produced a powerful new ship. They called it the *Pride of the South*.

They put it in the sea and sailed it back to shore, with Sally pointing from the poop deck and Pete steering into the sun. Sally said it was a pretty powerful partnership. Pete said he was surprised at the sense of it. And when they sailed the *Pride of the South* professionally and smoothly into the city harbor, Mayor Mitchell mustered the masses to a meeting, and Sally and Pete were both made meritorious mariners.

From then on, Spectacular Sally and Petroleum Pete pursued piracy as a pair, with a success that was something to be seen. Pete learned to say sentences with style, and Sally learned that she could pronounce phrases with precision. All worked out well. And it's a good thing too, because keeping Petroleum Pete practically perfect in his pronunciation, and surrounding Sally with scintillating sibilant syllables, would get anyone significantly pooped!

Enchanted

Once upon a time there was an enchantress who lived in a castle on the very top of a tall mountain. The view from the castle was beautiful, and the enchantress loved to stand on her balcony at sunset, imagining the wondrous places that lay in the far distance. When she wanted more than just the view, she would journey down into the small town at the foot of the mountain, where travelers from many countries would come to shop, meet, and share stories. She would wander among the crowds, listen to the babble of different languages, try exotic foods the travelers had brought, and dream of the time when she could travel to the far-off lands of which the minstrels sang.

It was during just such a visit that the enchantress met a powerful sorcerer. From the moment they met she liked what she saw. He was very handsome, with a long, immaculate velvet cloak and a confident smile. He liked her, too. He liked the way she was so excited to listen to the travelers' stories and learn of their different ways.

The enchantress and the sorcerer began to meet often, taking long walks, sitting in cafes, and drinking tea together. The more time they spent together, they more they fell in love. But as they loved each other more, they began to cast spells on each other.

You might ask, why did they cast spells on each other? Well, casting spells is simply what enchantresses and sorcerers do. It's how they get what they want. They have done it so often that they cast spells out of habit, almost without realizing it.

So, because she had liked him so much when they met, the enchantress cast a spell that made the sorcerer stay exactly as he was then, wearing the same cloak and the same confident smile. And because the sorcerer liked the way the enchantress was so excited and happy during her visits to the town, he cast a spell that kept her from going anywhere else.

Now, these spells were very subtle; there were no bright flashes or puffs of smoke or anything like that. It worked like this: If the sorcerer tried to put on anything but his velvet cloak, he would feel uncomfortable and itchy, like his clothes just didn't feel right. Only when he put on his velvet cloak would he feel at ease again. And when he saw the enchantress, if his face showed anything besides confidence, he would start to get a nervous feeling in the pit of his stomach until he put his confident smile back on his face. So even though he had lots of clothes and lots of different feelings, when he was with her, he always looked just the same.

It was similar for the enchantress. If she started to leave the town, even to go back to her castle, the spell would make her feel nervous and scared. The further she went, the more scared she felt, so eventually she rented a small house in town and didn't go back to her castle at all. She remembered, of course, that she used to wonder about far-off lands. But after a while she began to think that her dreams of visiting them were just that—dreams that would never be fulfilled. So even though she still liked hearing the travelers' tales, eventually, she stopped thinking about going outside the town at all.

The result? After several months, the enchantress and the sorcerer were fully and deeply in love—and were trapped in a web of spells that neither of them realized they were casting.

As time wore on, they continued to take walks and drink tea and love each other deeply, but they began to get more and more unhappy. The enchantress found herself wanting to see the sorcerer in different clothes, to see different expressions on his face. "He is always so much the same," she would think to herself, and she became very irritated with him for never changing—even though she was the one who had put the spell on him in the first place!

The sorcerer felt the same. He began to get tired of always being in the town, and he found himself wondering why the enchantress never wanted to go anywhere, why she had no ambition to explore the world. He began to get irritated with her for being so stuck in one place—even though he was the one who had put the spell on her to stay there.

So instead of enjoying their walks and their meals, the enchantress and the sorcerer found themselves arguing all the time, but not really knowing why or what to do about it.

After many weeks of this arguing, something had to happen. Early one morning, it did. The enchantress woke up after a vivid dream. In the dream, she was flying on a winged stallion, over mountains and lakes and valleys and cities, seeing wonders she had never even imagined. She was filled with excitement and happiness and a feeling of freedom that thrilled her to her very center. She woke up with that feeling still in her heart, and without really thinking about it, she ran outside and jumped onto the first horse she came upon. She rode out of the town, moving as fast as the horse could carry her.

Now, as you may know, breaking a spell that has been cast on you is very difficult. As the enchantress rode, she began to feel a terrible fear in the pit of her stomach. Thoughts of the disasters that could befall her flooded her head: robbers, villains, terrifying animals, tornadoes. She felt filled by self-doubt, as though voices in her head were saying, "No, no, no! Go back! Go back! This is wrong!" All of this was completely predictable, of course; this is what it's like to go against a spell. But spurred on by her dream, she continued to ride as fast as she could despite the fear tearing at her from inside.

In another part of the town, the sorcerer suddenly woke up in a panic. This was predictable, too; it is what happens when a spell you have cast is about to be broken. First you feel angry, though you don't know why. Then you feel powerless and frustrated. Then finally, you get more and more scared as the spell gets closer and closer to dissolving.

Running outside, the sorcerer found a horse and rode off after the enchantress, desperately trying to catch up with her so that he could re-cast his spell. He rode so swiftly and so hard that his cloak was torn by the wind, but he kept on, spurred on by his rising terror.

After an hour, he caught up with her at the top of a ridge outside the town. As he approached, he began to scream at the enchantress with rage and fear. He was preparing to cast another, even more powerful spell to stop her, when something stopped him in his tracks. The enchantress, sitting on her horse looking over a broad, wide valley, seemed utterly different from what he was used to. She was shuddering with the fears that the spell had created inside her, but at the same time, her face was alight with the new possibilities she sensed on the road beyond. Her whole being seemed vibrant and alive. Despite his anger and fear he was fascinated. He felt as if he were seeing her for the first time. He lost all desire to cast a new spell as he sat open-mouthed, looking at her.

At that moment, the enchantress turned to look at the sorcerer, and she too was struck by how different he seemed. His cloak was tattered and dirty. His face showed much more than just the confidence she had always loved; it showed fear, and anger, and longing, and most importantly, just how deeply he loved her. As she looked at him in all his confusion and complexity, she realized anew how much she loved him.

And in that brief but wonderful instant, the spells were broken and a transformation began. The enchantress seemed to grow. The sorcerer could almost see the depth and intensity of her thirst for adventure, as it filled her cheeks with color and her eyes with fire and her heart with longing. The sorcerer seemed to grow, too. His cloak began to shimmer and change into a thousand colors and styles. His voice deepened and sang, and he felt a tide of warmth sweep over him. Suddenly it was as if they were newly met again. And between them burned a flame of unquenchable love.

Because, you see, that's what happens when spells are broken. New possibilities rush in to fill the space left by the fear. It's not that enchantresses and sorcerers never try to cast spells again. Of course they do, because habits run deep. But the more they practice breaking the spells, the less power those spells have over them. And their lives become deeper and riskier and richer and more full than they could have ever dreamed.

So it was for the enchantress and the sorcerer. So may it be for all of us.

Adventure Calls

My name's Mike. I have to tell you about this weird experience I had the other day. First, let me tell you a little bit about myself. I live in a great apartment in a city. I've got a big television set right where I can see it. I've got a remote control, so I can sit on my couch and check all the channels I want without even having to move. I've got my cookies and my

drinks right where I can get to them. If I want to, I can shut the windows and draw the shades so I don't get any noise or any glare. In fact, if I want to, I can sit and watch television all day, every day.

See, I've always been the kind of guy who likes things to be predictable and calm. I never liked conflicts, or problems, or uncertainty, or anything like that. I've always liked things to be easy and smooth, and above all, comfortable. That's the way I want it. That's the way I always wanted it.

Like, if my friend Lee Ann were to call me up and ask me to do something, like take a walk in the park or go to a movie, I would tell her, "No way. That stuff's too dangerous. You never know what can happen to you on a walk in the park or on the way to a movie theater. It's dangerous out there! I'm sorry, but no. I like to stay right here where things are just the way I like them."

That's what used to happen. But one day not long ago, things changed big-time. I was sitting on my couch, minding my own business, eating cookies and watching television, when I felt a calling. It was my cell phone vibrating in my pocket. I thought maybe it was Lee Ann trying to convince me to do something, but when I answered, another woman's voice, soft and musical, said, "Michael, this is Adventure calling."

"What do you mean, Adventure calling? I don't know anybody named Adventure. Are you sure you have the right number?"

"Oh, yes," said the voice. "This is Adventure, and I'm calling for you. Great treasures await you, Michael. Excitement and explorations. Amazing experiences in far-off lands. You're never going to get anywhere if you stay in that concrete box of yours. You need to come out and find your destiny. It's not going to come in there and sit in your lap."

"But I don't want adventure and excitement!" I said. "I want ease and predictability. I want comfort and control. I want to stay here and watch TV with my drinks and cookies by my side!"

"Thank you for sharing, but that's not going to happen. See you soon." And she hung up.

Just as I put the phone back into my pocket, the walls began to quake and the floor began to shake. I tried to stand up, but the room seemed to be spinning.

"What could this be?" I thought. "A tornado? An earthquake?" I tried to run to the door, but the floor seemed to be rolling under my feet. I fell over and hit my head, and everything went dark.

Sometime later—I don't know how long—I woke up. Everything was different. I felt like I was gently swaying back and forth. I felt fresh air on my face. I sat up. Somehow, impossibly, I wasn't in my apartment anymore. I was in a huge, open boat. Big, sweaty guys in ripped T-shirts sat on benches all around me, grunting as they pulled on heavy oars.

All I could see in every direction was water. Suddenly, from nowhere, I heard a growly voice like out of an old pirate movie.

"Listen up, ye bunch of no-good deck-scrubbing swabbies! This is your captain speaking. You are on Pirate Boat Lines voyage #8752, en route to The Island of Perfect Unpredictability at an altitude of zero feet above sea level. Our lovely, well-trained staff will be happy to provide anything you need. Please keep your seats while we are at sea and do not stand up until the boat has come to a complete stop at the island. If ye do, ye'll surely walk the plank. Thank you and have a pleasant trip."

This didn't sound good at all. I looked around. The lovely, well-trained staff were more sweaty guys in ripped T-shirts slamming mugs of swill into people's hands. "No thanks," I thought. How did I get here? I don't like this! I want my couch! I want my TV! I want my cookies! I want to go home!

But there didn't seem to be much I could do. So I sat there for what seemed like hours, until finally, the boat came to a stop next to a big green island. Everyone was getting up, so I stood up too.

As I tried to figure out what to do next, a woman suddenly appeared. She was dressed in a long skirt and a dark blouse and a baseball cap. Her long, curly hair cascaded down her back.

She said brightly, "Well, Michael, I see you've made it. Now it's time to go!"

I recognized her voice. "You must be the one on the phone! What's the big idea here? I want to go home! How can I get home?"

And Adventure (because, of course, that's who she was) said, "Well, this boat is going even farther away, so pretty much your only option is to get off and explore the island and see if you can find the way home from there."

"But I don't wanna explore!" I cried. "I wanna go home!"

Adventure just looked at me with those big eyes of hers, and I realized I didn't have any choice.

"Okay, okay," I said, "I'll go to the island. How do I get there?"

"How do you get there?" she repeated, laughing. "You just step out of the boat and walk! It's not far, and the water's not that deep."

"Are you crazy? I'm not stepping in that water! It might be cold. It might be wet. There might be sea urchins or ana-menomies. Or squiddlies or clobsters. It could be dangerous!"

"I suppose that's true. This *is* the Water of Sleeping Unknowns, after all, so I suppose anything could happen. But you'll probably be fine."

Well, there didn't seem to be much choice, so I stepped into the water. As it turned out, once I was actually in it, the water was kind of nice. But I didn't know what might be there, so I ran through it as fast as I could.

Once I got onto the beach, I realized one thing. The sand was hot—Ooch! Ouch! Ow!

"Hey," I yelled to Adventure, who was somehow already waiting for me where the beach met the forest. "This sand is hot! What do I do?"

"This is The Beach of Temporary Discomfort," she called back. "The sand is a bit hot, but if you squish your toes into it, you'll get down to the cool sand."

I pushed my feet down into the sand, scrunching my toes deeper and deeper. Finally, the pain started to ease as I reached the cooler sand below. That was a lot better. I thought about staying there for a while, but that wouldn't get me anywhere. So I shuffled my feet across the beach to where Adventure was standing.

As I walked up to her, I realized that Adventure was in front of a dark and green jungle. I hadn't noticed it before because I was so focused on the water and the sand. It was a scary-looking jungle, with trees so thick that I couldn't see even ten feet inside it.

"I suppose you are going to tell me I have to go into this jungle," I said, hoping and hoping that she would say no.

"You don't *have* to do anything. But if you want to get home, it's either back into the ocean or through the Jungle of Imminent Chaos. It's your decision."

"Okay, okay," I said, "I get it." I didn't like the look of this at all, but I really wanted to get back to my couch and my TV and my cookies. So I headed into the jungle.

Now let me tell you, this place was creepy. The air was cool and damp. There were vines hanging from every tree. All around me, I could hear howls and cries of strange animals. In every nook and cranny, I thought I saw crouching beasts. I started walking, but every step I took seemed to create crackles and crunches and snaps in the undergrowth. I was sure I was waking up the terriblest of monsters. I thought I heard one behind me, and I started walking faster. Then I saw another one coming down from the treetops. I could feel the creepy crawly sticky feeling of a snake slithering down my back. I started to run, screaming "Help! Help! They're all after me!" I ran faster and faster, and then I tripped. I got up again and found myself pinned against a tree, and I knew this was it. I was going to die, the monsters were going to get me, and so I covered my head with my hands, ready to meet my doom!

And then, well, it's kind of embarrassing to say, but nothing happened. Nothing at all. I peeked out from between my fingers. The creepy animals were out there, but in fact, none of them was actually paying any attention to me. They were just going on about their usual creepy animal business.

"What a relief!" I thought. "What a miracle!" Then I stopped. "Wait a minute. What an insult! You didn't even notice I was there! What, I'm not good enough for you to eat? And you call yourselves monsters?"

I started walking again. I had no idea I was going to get insulted like that. I'm not even worth scaring? Hmmph.

After a few more uneventful minutes, I came out of the jungle at the foot of a broad, tall mountain. It looked so high, and I'd never climbed anything higher than a bunk bed in my whole life.

"How am I going to get up that?" I thought. I leaned against a big rock and closed my eyes.

"What's the problem?" asked Adventure, who had somehow shown up again.

"How am I going to get up this huge mountain?" I complained. "It has no paved paths or handrails!"

"Well, yes, that's true. This is the Mountain of Extreme Difficulty. The only way to get over it is to climb it."

Yet again, it didn't seem like I had a choice so I started up the mountain. First I found a rock that I could grab with my left hand. I started pulling myself up, bracing my right foot on a small ledge, thinking, "I don't want to do this! I want to be home with my remote control!" Then I found a handhold for my right hand and a place for my left foot, and I hoisted myself a little higher.

"I mean, who is this Adventure anyway? She drags me off my couch, puts me on that crazy pirate ship and on this weird island," (Here I found a crack where I could put both feet, so I got another ways up the mountain) "and then she says, like it's nothing at all, that I've got to climb this sky-scraper of a mountain," (I found another handhold; actually, this was getting a lot easier now) "like I've got nothing better to do than spend my time almost getting eaten by monsters" (I realized that if I twisted my foot a little sideways, my feet could grip the rock just about perfectly) "and wondering if I'll ever see my TV again." (I was kind of getting the hang of this, reaching with one hand and then the other, one foot and then the other) "I mean, it's so unfair that—wait, I'll bet if I can just reach a little higher, I can get up to that ledge. Yes! I can almost see the top now, let me just put my knee in this crevice, and, yep, that's right, almost there, all I need to do is just grab hold of that little outcropping, and, yep, almost, okay, I've got it. Yes! I made it to the top!"

I could hardly believe I was on top of the mountain. I looked back to where I had come from and thought, "I climbed that? Incredible!"

I turned around, and the view was breathtaking. As far as I could see in all directions were hills and valleys, covered in trees and dotted with meadows and streams. It looked like paintings I'd seen on TV documentaries about famous artists. But it was real! And down to my left, just on the other side of a slightly lower peak, I could see an emerald-green lake shimmering in the sun.

Well, I was hot and sweaty from the climb, and that lake looked like the most beautiful thing I could ever imagine. I was immediately seized with a desire to jump into it and swim, twisting and turning under the water with the sun's beams reflecting down through it. Still catching my breath from all the excitement, I asked Adventure, "What is that lake on the other side of that peak?"

And she answered, "That is the Lake of Endless Possibility. Quite amazing, isn't it?"

"It sure is. How do I get to it?"

"Well, you could climb down the other side of this mountain, go through the valley below, up that next mountain, and down its other side. Eventually, some time from now, you'd get to the lake. Or you could take the Rickety Bridge of Uncertainty."

I looked to where she pointed. A bridge? It looked like toothpicks tied together with two strands of dental floss!

"Walk across that?" I said. "Are you insane? It looks like it could fall apart any second!"

"Well, it hasn't fallen apart yet, and it's been here for a long time. But it's up to you. What do you want to do?"

"What do you mean?"

"Just what I said. I can't tell you which way to go. There are some places in your life where you have to make your own decisions, and here, on the Peak of Ultimate Responsibility, is one of them. You can take the long but sure way, or you can take the Rickety Bridge of Uncertainty and go the short but exciting way. It's your choice."

So what could I do? I looked at the bridge. I was terrified. But to tell the truth, there was something kind of exciting about that rickety bridge. It looked like it would probably hold. And if I made it across, I would be on the top of that next peak, and the Lake of Endless Possibility would be just on the other side, waiting for me.

The next minute I found myself stepping onto the Rickety Bridge of Uncertainty. As I walked, it swung back and forth. I was hundreds of feet up in the air. It was like I was walking in space—scary, terrifying, but great! Step after step I went until, believe it or not, I made it to the other side.

When I got there, I found something I had never expected. On the top of the mountain was a platform with a U-shaped tube and water running down it. Yes—it was the Water Slide of Utter Uncontrollability!

This time I didn't even hesitate. I ran up to that water slide and jumped feet first onto it. Down I went, faster and faster and faster. I had no way of steering, no way of stopping, no way of doing anything but going faster and faster down the slide. The only thing I could do was yell, and so I did. "Yeeeaaahooooo!"

I sailed down for what seemed like forever, and then suddenly the slide ended. I flew into the air and came down with a humongous splash right into the Lake of Endless Possibility.

The water was cool and clear, filled with green and blue light. I twisted and turned and swam and flipped. I felt the ebbing and flowing of the currents, possibilities swirling around me. I was so comfortable, so relaxed, so excited, so amazed. I came up to the surface to take a big breath of air.

And somehow, impossibly, I was back in my own living room, on my couch with my cookies and remote control by my side. Everything was quiet except for the people talking on the TV.

This was awful. I jumped up. "Hey! What happened? Where's the water? Where's the lake?" But there was no one to answer.

I fell onto the couch again. How could this be? I was just rocketing down the Water Slide of Utter Uncontrollability, and then I splashed into the lake, and then I was swimming, and it was so great! I want to go back! How can I go back?

My phone was ringing. I pulled it out of my pocket, feeling like I was in a dream. Maybe this was Adventure calling again!

"Hello!" I said. "Adventure, is that you? I want to go back to the Lake of Endless Possibility! How do I get there?"

It wasn't Adventure. It was Lee Ann again, asking if I wanted to go for a walk in the park. Like I said, she asks me this pretty often, and I usually say no, because, well, you know, you can get dirty out there, and you never know how much traffic you are going to hit, and . . . .

I looked at the phone again, and I realized that maybe it *was* Adventure calling, after all. So I put the phone back up to my ear and said, "Yeah, that sounds great!"

Maybe Adventure will call you sometime too!

Happily Ever After? Yeah, Right!

This story is about a girl named Cinderella. You may remember her; she had a terrible family, with a mean stepmother, two nasty stepsisters, and a house that constantly needed cleaning. And you know what happened. Cinderella somehow lived through this difficult childhood, went to the ball, met Prince Charming, who fell in love with her, and they got married. And then? Of course! They lived happily ever after!

Yeah, right! Actually, it was a lot more complicated. You see, after she got married to Prince C., Cinderella went to live at the castle. Eventually the prince became King Charming, and Cinderella became queen. They had three kids: a daughter named Gwendolyn, a son named Jeffrey, and the youngest one, Sophie. It's true that they lived pretty well; they were the royal family, after all. But they didn't exactly live "happily" ever after. And the reason? They worried a lot.

Take King Charming. There he was, the big cheese, the ruler of the whole kingdom. You would think that he would feel great. But no. He wasn't happy at all. You see, one thing made him very, very scared, and he worried about it every day. Know what it was? He was afraid of talking in front of large groups. Oh, he could talk to one or two people, no problem. But if he had to make a speech in front of the whole court, or the army, or the town merchants or somebody like that, he would worry himself sick. He was afraid that he would forget what he was going to say, or that he would make a mistake and say something dumb, and everyone would laugh at him. He couldn't even sleep, he worried so much. As a result, he stayed home almost all the time so he wouldn't have to talk to anyone. The army never really knew what it was supposed to do, and the people of the kingdom wondered what was going on. And King Charming was miserable.

Cinderella wasn't much better. She worried about getting a cold. Because she was sure that if she got a cold, it would turn into pneumonia, or bronchitis, or eczema, or halitosis, or something deadly anyway, and that would be it for her. So Cinderella used all of her queenly powers to avoid getting sick. She wouldn't go out when it was cold. She wouldn't go out when it was cool. She wouldn't go out even when it was warm, because it might get cold. She wouldn't let her children go out either, because she was afraid they might bring germs into the castle. She even decreed that no one in the whole kingdom could go outside in the winter, just in case they might spread germs. But it didn't work. Even with all the kingdom's people inside, still she worried every day that she might get sick.

The kids had worries too. Princess Gwendolyn was deathly afraid of fire and anything with fire in it, like candles, campfires, and barbecues. She worried that if anyone ever lit a candle inside, the castle would burn to the ground. She even convinced her dad to decree that no one in the kingdom could light a fire, even on the coldest nights, just to make sure. But still she worried all the time.

Prince Jeffrey was afraid of monsters. There was one under the bed that made him shiver. There was one that lived in the closet that was horrible. But the one that worried him the absolute most was the ketchup monster. You

see, Jeffrey's Aunt Driselda had once told him a story about this red, slimy monster with huge fangs and bubbly hair that lives in ketchup bottles. She said that one day when he least expected it, he would open a bottle of ketchup to put some on his french fries, and pop! out would come the ketchup monster to eat him up with one big burp. Ever since, Jeffrey had been afraid of that monster, and he would lie awake at night worrying about whether anyone had snuck ketchup into the castle that day. Eventually the king had to decree that no ketchup could be eaten anywhere in the kingdom. But Jeffrey still worried.

What about Sophie, the youngest? Well, she was a pretty regular kid. The thing she worried about most was that her family was bizarre. And you can see why she would worry about that.

The Charming family lived like this for a long time, until one year, Festival Day came around. Festival Day was the biggest holiday in all the kingdom. It was held only once every fifty years, and it was a very special tradition that had been around since the founding of the kingdom thousands of years ago. On that day, all the people of the kingdom would come from far and wide to have a huge party and picnic on the castle grounds. They would dance and sing all afternoon. Then just at dinnertime, the royal family would come out of the castle and walk into the crowd. The king would make a speech, and everybody would hug and kiss the queen. Then everyone would fire up their barbecues, and there would be hot dogs and french fries and ketchup for all!

That was the ancient tradition. The people of the kingdom expected it.

Now, you can imagine how the royal family felt about this. The king was terrified, the queen was mortified, Princess Gwendolyn was horrified, and Prince Jeffrey was petrified!

And Little Sophie? She was worried, too. She was worried that all the people would be out there waiting, and her family's worries would wreck the celebration!

Sure enough, when Festival Day came and all the people were gathered outside the castle, the royal family was nowhere to be found. Sophie searched and searched. Finally she found them sitting in the throne room, too paralyzed with fear to move.

"Come on!" she said. "The people are all out there! What are you waiting for? It's time to go outside!"

"We can't," Cinderella said. "We're scared!"

"What kind of a family is this?" said Sophie. "Dad won't go anywhere there are people. Mom thinks she's going to die from a cold. Gwen won't move if she thinks there's fire anywhere. And Jeff won't move if there's any sign of ketchup! All the while the people are saying, 'Why won't the king speak to us? Why can't we go out and build fires in the winter? And why can't anyone eat french fries anymore?' This is no way to run a kingdom!"

There was a silence, and then they all answered at once.

"But what if I forget what I'm going to say?" said King Charming.

"But what if I get a cold?" said Cinderella.

"But what if the castle catches fire?" said Gwendolyn.

And Jeffrey said, "But what if the ketchup monster crawls

out of the ketchup bottle, and eats us all up, and then eats up the castle, and then eats up the kingdom, and then eats up the world, and then the planets, and then the galaxies, and then the *universe*?"

There was a silence. Everybody was kind of stunned. They looked at Jeffrey, and then at each other.

"Well," said King Charming, chuckling, "that's not really likely to happen, is it, Jeffrey? I mean, eating up the whole universe?"

"Well, you are probably not going to forget what you are going to say anyway, Dad. You never do when you're talking to us!" said Gwendolyn, giggling.

"Well, Gwendolyn," said Cinderella, laughing, "the castle is probably not going to burn down either, since it's made of stone."

"And even if you get a cold, Mom," said Sophie, "you probably won't die, even if you *do* get halitosis. People get colds all the time."

There was a pause while everyone thought.

And then Cinderella said, "You know, you're right. We've got a kingdom to run. We've got people who need us out there. We can't just sit here. We'd better go out anyway, fears and all. If we all go together, maybe we'll be all right."

So they stood up together, Queen Cinderella, King Charming, Gwendolyn, Jeffrey, and Sophie. They linked arms and walked out into the sunshine of the courtyard, and the crowd of citizens rushed to greet them.

From that day on, they did live pretty happily ever after.

Oh, the king did forget what he was going to say a couple of times, but he always made something up, and no one laughed. After all, he was the king! Cinderella did catch cold a few times, but she just sat home and watched Oprah until she was better, so that wasn't so bad. Gwendolyn became a Girl Scout and got a merit badge for campfire making. Sophie, who always had good ideas, became an advisor to the royal court. And it must be said that since that day, the ketchup monster has never been seen in that kingdom again.

But . . . the ketchup monster could be anywhere. So you might want to be just a little bit careful the next time you eat french fries!

Reduce, Re-use, Recycle

This is the story of James Crickle. It is a tale of reexamining a life, of losing and finding a self, of near-panic, and finally, of reconnection. It is a tale to be told and retold.

James lived in Rehoboth and worked in a reupholstering factory. His job was to reattach the legs to recliners after they had been reupholstered, and to reglue and refurbish couches when they needed repair. James found it relaxing; he left work each day feeling refreshed and ready to resume his recreational activities, like reading. James relished his job and felt like he was a responsible and respectable citizen.

One day, when James arrived at work, he found that his quiet life of reupholstering and refurbishing was about to be totally rearranged. His boss informed him that he had been removed from his job.

James's reaction was one of shock. "What?" he said. "I've been rejected? How can that be? My reattaching can't be beat! My regluing is renowned! What can be the reason?"

"We've decided not to repair anything anymore," the boss said. "Reusing and repairing? Part of the past. We've decided to use only things that are new, and so we're going to reduce the size of our workforce. I'm sorry, but you'll just have to resign."

James was crushed. He walked out onto the sidewalk. "How can I recover from this?" he asked himself. "How will I rebuild my life? I'm too young to retire and too old to retrain. I'll be restricted to receiving unemployment. And they'll probably repossess my car!"

With terrible sadness, James sat down on a bench to review his options. "I need help," he reflected. "I need someone to help me reclaim my job." And then across the street,

he saw it. "City Hall!" he said to himself. "That's the place I should go! Maybe someone there can help me redress these wrongs and reconstruct my life. Or maybe I can at least get some revenge!"

So James walked into City Hall. There were hundreds of doors on each side of a long hallway. "Which one should I choose?" He walked along the hall until he saw a door marked "Lost and Found."

"That might work," he said to himself. He opened the door and went in.

The office was small and cozy. It had movie posters all over the walls: "Lost in Space," "Lost Horizons," "Raiders of the Lost Ark," "Lost World," and "Lost of the Mohicans."

James was standing there wondering about that last one when a man rushed up to him with an excited smile. "Yes? Yes? Can I help you?" he said earnestly. "Did you lose something? Did you find something? Oh, I'm so excited to see you!"

"Well," said James, "I . . ."

"You see," the man continued, barely listening to James, "we here in the Lost and Found Office just *love* losing and finding things! Have you lost your marbles? Your wits? Your senses? Have you lost touch or lost interest? Or maybe you've just lost perspective?"

"Well, no," said James, somewhat flustered. "I mean, well, yes. I just lost my job."

"Excellent," the man answered breathlessly, "excellent!" He took out a notepad and began scribbling furiously. "Now, where did you last put it?"

"Put what?" asked James.

"Your job, your job!" said the man.

"Well, just where it always was, I guess," James answered.

"Excellent!" said the man. "And when did you last see it?"

"Well, this morning," said James. "But I don't think you understand. I know where the job is, I just . . . "

"But . . . but I thought you said you'd *lost* it," said the man, his face falling. "If you know where it is, then you didn't lose it. Oh, this is terrible! We'll be no help to you at all!" The man totally lost control of himself and began crying. Then suddenly he looked up at James and said, "I'm sorry, forgive me. Now, what were we talking about? I seem to have lost track."

James stared at him. "Oh, nothing," he said. "I'll find my way out." He hurried out into the hall. "You could lose your sanity in there, that's for sure," he said to himself, as he closed the door.

James went on down the corridor. A little ways down he saw a door marked "Don't Panic." He said to himself, "That sounds like an office for someone who has just lost his job. Maybe they can help me."

He opened the door. This room couldn't have been more different from the last one. It was brightly lit and full of people and activity. At one end, there was a huge panoramic map of Panama. At the other end, there was an enormous stove covered with frying pans and piles of fresh pancakes. And in the middle of the room was a large box of enormous pansies.

James was about to look for someone to talk to when, suddenly, pandemonium broke out. A large panda dressed in panties burst into the room and headed towards the pancakes. At the same time, a panther wearing pants burst through a pane of glass next to the panorama of Panama. The people around the pancakes panicked, and several jumped into the pansies. The panda and the panther started a kind of pantomime (with some panache, actually), when suddenly from behind a panel jumped a figure all dressed in green. (It must be, James realized, Peter Pan.) Peter Pan chased the panther and the panda away from the pancakes and then ran up to James.

"We can help you cope with panic!" Peter Pan panted. James, however, backed out of the room and closed the door. This was one Pandora's box he didn't care to open.

He stood for a moment, thinking that City Hall wasn't going to be much help after all. But as he turned to leave, he caught sight of a door he hadn't noticed before. This one said, "Reduce, Reuse, Recycle."

"Hm," James thought. "That sounds interesting." Curious, he opened the door and went inside.

Suddenly he felt like he had returned home. The air had a refined quality. He felt refreshed, like he was reexperiencing a place that had long ago receded into memory.

A pleasant-looking woman walked up to him. "Welcome," she said in a warm voice, "to Reduce, Reuse, and Recycle. Can I help you?"

"Well," said James, "I don't know. This morning I was

rejected from my job repairing recliners, and my reaction, of course, was to seek revenge, and . . ."

"You're one of us!" the woman suddenly shouted. "I'd recognize that kind of retelling anywhere! Come in, come in! We're so glad you have revealed yourself!" She grabbed James's arm and started pulling him across the room. "I can't tell you how good it is to have you here."

"What do you mean?" James asked her as he was dragged along. "Who are you?"

"We're the reduce, reuse, recycle crew, of course!" said the woman. "Everyone here is dedicated to reducing, reusing, and recycling. Let me introduce you. Penelope here reduces her use of water by washing her clothes only once every two weeks and her dishes only once every month. She smells a bit repulsive and eating off the dishes is repugnant, but it's like a religion to her, and she can't resist! Danny reuses his newspapers. He gets kind of bored reading the same ones over and over again of course, but it's really important to him. He also reuses his paper towels and his dental floss! And Linda here recycles stuff—old cardboard boxes into hamster cages, old milk cartons into pots for plants, and pencil shavings into stuffing for pillows. Isn't that great! Sit down, sit down!" she continued, bubbling over with enthusiasm.

She sat James down at a table, reached into a cupboard, and brought out some plates. "The table's been recently refurbished," she said, "and the chair has been reconstructed from the remnants of recycled recliners, just like the kind you used to repair!" She came over to the table and continued,

"Here's some refried beans that I just reheated. The plate is made from recycled plastic. And if you want more hot chocolate, you can always have a refill!"

"Now," she went on, "we all reside together. I hope you'll agree to remain with us. We are a bit reclusive, I suppose, but we respect each other. And if you remain with us, you'll never be rejected again."

James sat and reflected for a moment. The woman was right. James belonged here. Just sitting at this refinished table, watching the people reducing, reusing, and recycling, made him feel renewed, refreshed, reinvigorated. His thoughts of revenge and retaliation receded, and a feeling of relaxation came over him. "This really is the place for me," he reasoned. "I see no reason to retreat."

When the woman came back, James said, "I have reflected on it, and with high regard for your reputation and your respectability, I will not resist. I will remain."

"I'm so relieved!" cried the woman. She ran to tell the others, and everyone rejoiced.

And James has remained a reliable and respected resident of Reduce, Reuse, Recycle ever since. He has helped them repair, refurbish, rearrange, and reconstruct a remarkable range of things. No more being lost or found for James and no more panic. James is where he belongs.

And the moral of the story, of course, is that no matter how rejected, repelled, or repudiated we might feel, each of us has people we can respect and relax with. We just have to find them. Really.

Sunny Side Mary

In a medium-sized town not far from here, there was a middle school. It was just like any other middle school, except for two things. First, instead of an auditorium, it had a courtyard, a huge round covered area right in the center of the school. In the middle of the courtyard was a big round pool with fountains and lights. Right in the middle of the pool was a circular stage, connected to one side of the courtyard by a narrow bridge.

The kids who went there liked having the only school with a round stage; it was very cool.

But there was one problem. Whenever there was a concert, half of the kids would always have to look at the performers' backs. Plus, that side of the courtyard didn't have very good lights, and it was always a little bit cold. Because of this, everyone called that part the shady side, while the other part of the courtyard was called the sunny side. Now, it wouldn't be too bad to have a sunny side and a shady side, if the kids sometimes got to be on one side and sometimes on the other. But that's not the way it was.

That's the second thing that was different about this school. Some kids in the school came from the North Side of town and some from the South Side. And there was a rule: during concerts in the courtyard, only the North Side kids could sit on the sunny side. The South Side kids had to sit on the shady side.

What would happen if a South Side kid went onto the sunny side? It was always the same. The North Side kids would just pick her up and dump her into the fountain. And if she came back, they'd just keep dumping her into the fountain until she went back to her side. It was pretty awful.

You're probably wondering exactly who made up this crazy rule. Well, no one exactly knows. The North Side kids always said that the principal had made the rules and they were just doing what she said. So besides getting to sit on the sunny side, the North Side kids got to feel important, too, because they figured they were doing what the grownups wanted. However, if you asked the principal, she would say that it was the kids' choice, and that the South Side kids actually *liked* to be on the shady side because they were used to it. And what if you talked to the teachers? Well, some of them would say that the North Side kids behaved better than the other kids, and so the North Side kids *should* be on the sunny side. Besides, they would say, it was natural for kids to divide up like that. There were some other teachers who would say that it probably shouldn't be that way. But none of them did anything to change it.

So the school was a great place to be, *if* you were from the North Side. But if you were from the South Side, it wasn't so great. It wasn't just that you couldn't really see what was going on during concerts. What was really upsetting was knowing that you couldn't go over to the other side, because if you did, you'd get thrown in the fountain. It just didn't seem fair.

Things went on like that for a long time, until the day that Mary went wading. A big concert was planned for lunchtime that day, with a band called the Zoot Suit Tooters. Mary had been waiting to see this particular band for a long time. She was a huge Zoot Suit Tooters fan. She had all the Tooters CDs and T-shirts, and she had their posters plastered all over the walls of her bedroom. They were her absolutely favorite group. But Mary was a South Side kid so she knew she was going to have to sit on the shady side and not see the front of the band at all. That made her angry.

So Mary decided to do something different. She planned it all out. On the day of the concert, she got to the courtyard early and found a place to sit on the sunny side. Over and over, she said to herself, "I don't care what they do or what they say, I am not moving. The Tooters are my favorite band, and I am going to see them from the front, no matter what."

Well, it came time for the assembly, and the North Side kids started showing up. Of course, the first thing they saw was Mary sitting on their side. And what do you think they did? First they just looked at her like she was crazy. Mary didn't move.

Then they said, "Hey South Sider, get over on your side of the courtyard!"

Mary just pretended not to hear them. They yelled louder. They called her names. They stared at her and told her to move, or else. And still Mary ignored them. So what did they do? A bunch of the biggest North Side kids picked her up and threw her in the fountain with a big splash!

Mary did not like that at all. She stood up in the water, dripping. She wasn't hurt, since the pool wasn't that deep—only up to her waist or so—and the water was pretty warm. But she did *not* like being thrown out of her seat. It made her angry. She glared at the North Side kids. They glared back.

Mary stepped out and went back to where she was sitting. The North Side kids threw her into the fountain again. She got up and went back to her seat. They threw her back in the fountain. She got up again, and as she got out of the fountain, they started to come after her . . . so she *walked* back into the fountain. It was better than getting thrown in, anyway.

Mary sat down in the water and thought, "This is awful! Here I am, soaking wet. If I ask the teachers to help, they'll just say that I should have stayed on my side. If I ask the principal, she'll just say that I should like the shady side better. Nobody's going to help me. What am I going to do?"

Finally, she stood up, feeling totally defeated. She started walking through the fountain back toward the shady side—slosh, slosh, slosh. As she walked, the rhythm of her feet reminded her of a song that her grandmother used to sing. It went like this:

Wade in the water
Wade in the water, children,
Wade in the water,
God's gonna trouble the water.

With that song flowing over and over again in her head, she realized with a giggle that, believe it or not, she actually *was* wading in the water! She looked at the shady side and all the South Side kids there. She looked at the stage, and she thought about the song. And she thought to herself, "Wait a minute. If wading in the water is good enough for God, it's good enough for me!"

And you know what Mary did? She turned right around and started sloshing back to where she had started.

Wade in the water
Wade in the water, children,
Wade in the water,
God's gonna trouble the water.

As she hummed the song and bounced along with the rhythm, the strangest thing happened. Somehow the other South Side kids must have heard the song. They got up from where they were sitting, and they walked into the fountain, too. Slosh, slosh, slosh, slosh, all together! Mary sloshed back toward the sunny side, and the other South Side kids followed. And wouldn't you know it, just as they all got to the front of the stage, the Zoot Suit Tooters ran across the bridge and onto the stage, and the concert started. Mary and the other South Side kids were on the sunny side, in the water.

The North Side kids were stunned. They had never seen anything like this. They didn't know what to do. They couldn't throw the South Side kids into the fountain because they were already *in* the fountain—with the best view of the concert. It was wrong! The North Side kids looked at each other, and then they all rushed into the fountain to get in front of the South Side kids. They had to be first! They were *always* first! So they pushed, and shoved, and squirmed, and finally they got themselves right up to the front, squished right up next to the stage, where no one could be in front of them. The Zoot Suit Tooters were playing practically right over their heads, and . . . and . . . and they looked around and suddenly realized that while they were struggling to get in front of the South Side kids, the South Side kids had all gotten out of the fountain and were now sitting in the seats on the sunny side, drying off!

The North Side kids were stunned again. What could they do? They were in the fountain, and the South Side kids had all the best seats, with Mary right in front. There was no way the North Side kids could throw all the South Side kids in the fountain at once. The teachers and principal were speechless. The Zoot Suit Tooters played, and the South Side kids listened, and there wasn't much else the North Side kids could do. They sloshed over to the shady side to dry off. And that's where they sat to watch the concert.

Things were different in that school from then on. The principal learned that if she made crazy rules, people wouldn't follow them. The teachers learned that the South Side kids didn't want to be behind the stage all the time. The North Side kids learned that if they wanted to get a good seat at an assembly, they had to get there early. The South Side kids learned that if you all stand up together for something that is right, sometimes you can win. And because Mary had helped the South Side kids get a place on the sunny side, all her friends began to call her Sunny Side Mary, the name they call her to this very day.

One Flower
in a Field

Once upon a time there was a field. It had dry grass and thistles, and high places and low places, and some rocks scattered around, and a stream that passed through one side. And scattered about the field, here and there, were flowers. Buttercups and tulips, coneflowers and lupines, flowers of red, yellow, blue, and purple—all kinds of bright, beautiful flowers growing up out of the dry grass.

Now you may ask, how were these flowers growing when the field was so dry? The answer is that next to every flower there was a hole in the ground. And in each hole lived an animal whose job it was to tend that flower. Most were rabbits, but there were hedgehogs and field mice and even a badger or two. Every day each animal would come out of its hole, walk down to the stream, and use a leaf to scoop up some water. Then each would carry the leaf back and water the flower with it. And that's how the flowers grew.

And in a little gully in the field, next to a tall sunflower, lived a rabbit. Like all the other animals, every day she would go down to the stream and get some water for her sunflower. She loved that flower; it was tall and bright, strong and healthy, and she took very good care of it. Her other rabbit friends took care of their flowers, too, and she would often visit with them. Well, one day she was heading home after a visit, when she decided to hop up to the top of a little hill on the other side of her gully. When she got to the top, she saw something she had never seen before. Down in another little valley a ways away she saw a flower, a daisy. But this flower looked in bad shape. It was drooping, and its colors were fading.

Now, why had she never seen that flower before? It's not that big a mystery. She had just never hopped in that direction. All of her friends' homes happened to be in the other direction, so that's where she always went. Of course, she

knew that there were other flowers out there, and she had heard that there were some that weren't doing quite as well as the flowers where she lived. But she'd never actually seen one that looked as bad as this.

She hopped down the hill to take a closer look. And as she got a bit closer, she began to understand. This flower badly needed water. Its petals were beginning to wilt in the heat, and the ground all around its stem was parched and dry. She looked at it, feeling terrible that a flower could be that unhealthy and that neglected, and then she did . . . nothing.

She was thinking to herself that even though the flower looked so awful, it was just one flower in a field, after all. There were lots of others that were doing fine. She had enough work watering her own flower to worry about this one. So she went home and got on with her business, getting up every day, going to the stream, watering her flower, and visiting with her friends.

But the other flower didn't go away. Now, every day when she came home, she couldn't help but hop up to the top of the hill and take a quick look to see if it was looking any better. And every day it continued to look dry and wilted and droopy.

It started to get to her. She found herself thinking about that flower at night while she was trying to sleep. She found herself thinking about it in the morning when she was going off to the stream for water. She found she couldn't even enjoy her own flower as much, knowing that the other flower was wilting more and more every day.

Now, you may be wondering why she didn't just go over and water the flower. After all, it was just on the other side of the hill, and the stream had plenty of water. Well, that's a good question. She thought about it all the time. She'd think about making an extra trip to the stream to get some water for that flower. But then she'd think, "Well, you don't just march into someone's front yard and water their flower without asking, do you? What if they don't want you to water it? They might yell at you or something, and that would be terrible." Or "What if the flower likes being kind of dried-up and droopy? That's possible, isn't it?" Or "Aren't there animals whose job it is to go around and help out flowers whose owners don't water them?" Maybe she should leave it to them, because they know what to do, right? She wouldn't want to mess up their plans!

With all these questions swirling in her head, for a long time she just went about her business, taking care of her own flower every day and trying not to think about the wilting one. But it kept bothering her, especially at night. It was kind of irritating, actually. Sometimes she wished the flower would either just get better or die. But every time she sneaked a peek, it still looked as dry and droopy as ever.

Finally, she couldn't stand it any longer. "Flowers are just not supposed to be like that," she thought to herself. Flowers are supposed to be colorful and bright and beautiful. And so one day, on her way back home with a leaf full of water for her flower, she found herself hopping over the hill towards the dry flower instead.

As she got to the top of the hill, some of her friends called to her; they had been coming to visit and saw her hopping away. They asked where she was going, and she told them that she just had to water this other flower; she couldn't stand it anymore. They tried to convince her to come back. They said it might be dangerous over there, and she shouldn't be watering other people's flowers. But she kept on going. She hopped over the hill and down the other side.

And as she got close to the dry flower, a hedgehog suddenly popped out of a hole in the ground next to it. The hedgehog said, "Hey! What are you doing?"

And the rabbit said, "I'm going to water this flower. It's dry and wilting, and if I don't water it, it will die!"

The hedgehog said, "What business is it of yours whether this flower dies? This is my flower, and I'll take care of it how I want. You go home and take care of your own flower."

But the rabbit answered, "I'm sorry, but I tried that. Flowers are supposed to be bright and beautiful, not wilting and droopy. So I'm going to water this flower."

And she hopped right past the hedgehog, who continued to fuss and mumble and give her mean looks. She poured the water right at the base of the flower, and then she turned around and hopped back up the hill.

The next day, she came back and watered it again.

And the day after that, she watered it again.

And then another day, and another, and another. Her friends continued to say that she was crazy. And the hedgehog continued to yell at her whenever she got near. But the flower started to look better. First some of the color came back into the petals. Then it started to stand up a little straighter. Then its leaves started to fill out and get bigger. And then the flower even started to grow a little taller.

And strangely enough, as this flower got brighter and healthier and taller and more beautiful, so did the rabbit's own flower. And so did all the other flowers, all around the field, even ones that she never watered. The whole field started to brighten up, as the colors of the flowers got more vivid and the flowers stood up taller. It was almost as if there was more water everywhere.

How could that be? Is it that other rabbits started sneaking around and watering other people's flowers, too? Or is it that when someone waters a wilting flower somewhere, all flowers grow just a little brighter?

Who knows? Maybe we'll just have to try it and see.

The Storyteller by the Sea

The Storyteller by the Sea was known all around the world. Not many people had actually seen her because she lived on a far-off island. But lots of people had heard about the amaz-

ing stories she told. Stories of danger and courage that made people's hearts pound and their palms sweat. Stories of deep soul journeys that made people give up everything they had and enter a life of helping others. Stories of mystery and suspense so intense that one time, when she fell asleep in the middle of telling one, the entire audience waited for eight hours until she woke up again to hear how it all turned out. Stories so funny that people had to be given oxygen because they would laugh so hard that they couldn't breathe. The Storyteller, people said, could stop wars, could make people fall in love, inspire great works of art—just by telling stories, sitting on some palm fronds under a tree on a far-away island.

One time a group of admirers came to visit. They had heard about the Storyteller, and they wanted to hear first-hand some of the amazing stories she told. So they traveled from Asia and South America, from Africa and North America and Europe, all the way across the Pacific Ocean to the small island where the Storyteller lived. They came to her village and went out onto the beach to the spot where the Storyteller told her stories every night. They found some palm fronds to sit on, and they waited for her to arrive.

When the sun finally began to disappear over the water to the west, a woman emerged from one of the houses and began to walk over to the group. She had long, dark hair braided down her back. She was wearing a loose-fitting skirt and a blouse covered with prints of exotic-colored flowers. With her came a thin man carrying a large platter of fresh fruit slices.

The Storyteller sat down on her mat, facing the sun and the water. She looked at the travelers, who looked back at her expectantly. She opened her mouth as if to speak and then reached for a slice of pineapple. She chewed it thoughtfully. She sat and looked out at the ocean again.

They all sat like that for a while, until one of the travelers spoke up.

"O Storyteller, we have journeyed from around the world to visit you. We have heard of the stories you tell, and the wars you have stopped, and the couples who have fallen in love just by listening to your stories. Will you speak to us? Will you tell us one of your stories?"

The Storyteller sat for a moment. Then she leaned over and whispered into her assistant's ear. He nodded and said, "The Storyteller has so many stories that she does not know where to begin. Perhaps you have a suggestion or a request?"

"I do, I do!" said one of the travelers excitedly. "How about the story of the two alligators? That's the one where these two baby alligators are living happily in a swamp in Florida until they get captured by a group of college students from Minneapolis on spring break. The students sneak the alligators back to Minnesota in their backpacks and put them into an aquarium. Then the alligators escape. Since it's Minnesota, it's freezing outside, so they try to find the warmest place they can, which turns out to be the college president's hot tub. He comes out to sit in it one night and lowers himself into the hot water. He's relaxing and feeling great, when suddenly he feels the alligators crawling up his legs. He's so startled that he jumps up, straight out of the hot tub, straight out of his swimming suit, and he ends up standing there with no clothes on in the freezing weather, yelling and waking up the entire neighborhood! That was so funny! And then he realizes what has happened, and he thinks it would make a good joke, and he takes the alligators to the pool at the college where the swim team practices, and . . . and the swim coach . . . when she sees the alligators swimming with her swim team . . . she . . . she . . . ." The traveler was laughing so hard at the memory of the story that he couldn't even finish what he was saying.

The Storyteller laughed, too; she remembered that story. She opened her mouth to begin telling it when another traveler interrupted, "Wait, wait. What about the story of the two young lovers in Thailand? That's the one where the boy and the girl fall in love when they are ten years old, but then their parents marry them off to other people, and they have to live next door to each other for their whole lives. Can you imagine that, the two of them loving each other so desperately but never being able to kiss or hug or touch each other or even be alone together? Oh, my heart just breaks when I hear that story. It makes me want to love my husband and my kids better every time I hear it. Tell that one, if you would, please. It really changed my life."

The Storyteller nodded in understanding at the memory of that deeply powerful story. She opened her mouth to speak, but another traveler interrupted, saying, "Oh, I know what you mean. It's like that story of the girl in Argentina who wanted to be an airplane pilot. Do you remember that one? She wanted so badly to be a pilot that she actually built her own airplane as a high school science project, and then flew it way out over the mountains of Patagonia. But then that big storm came up, and she crashed and had to travel back over the mountains all by herself. That was so scary. When she finally got back home, she was so excited about having achieved her dream that even the weeks of hardship in the mountains didn't matter. When I heard that story, I thought how great it would be to be so devoted that you were willing to put everything you have into making something happen. I actually changed jobs because I was so inspired to try something I really wanted to do."

An excited conversation broke out among the travelers; apparently a lot of them had heard that story too. The Storyteller listened to them talk of hearing stories and feeling their lives changed by them. Eventually she held up her hand to quiet them and was about to speak when another of the travelers suddenly said, "You know what I think is the most amazing story? It's the one that the Storyteller tells that makes people never see their enemies the same way again. That story has stopped wars."

"Which one is that?" the others all asked at once. "Is it the one about the space colony on Mars? Or the one about the kids trapped in the Ukrainian coal mine? Or the one about the kangaroo colony in Australia?" The Storyteller was about to say something, but she saw that it was useless, and the first traveler answered, "No, no, it's the one about the two childhood friends. What happens is this: As children, they play together, build forts, climb trees, and take lots of hikes out in the woods. They especially like to pretend that they're animals, and they chase each other through the woods roaring and howling. But then they grow older and lose track of each other. Eventually, they get involved in politics, and they end up in rival groups. Things in their country get more and more tense, until the political parties begin to collect weapons and threaten to have a civil war. The two friends end up being leaders of their groups. One day, when things are so bad that it looks like violence is about to break out, they meet, each with a gun in his hand, in front of an angry, armed mob on the steps of a government building. It looks like the war is going to start right then and there, until one of the friends looks at the other, and something strange happens. He sees his old friend begin to shift and change. First his friend becomes a wolf with fangs bared, chasing a deer. Then he becomes an otter sliding down a riverbank into the water. Then he becomes a mother leopard nursing her cubs. And then the friend becomes a child, as he was when they first met. And then God speaks with the child's voice, saying, 'I am you.' And the man who is seeing all this drops his gun, and it falls to the ground. Then the gun falls from his friend's hand too. Everyone standing nearby can feel that something has happened, but they don't know what. The friends turn from each other to look at the crowd, and God begins to speak in one voice after another, saying, 'I am you,' 'I am you,' 'I am you,' until it becomes a murmur that flows over and throughout the whole crowd. The guns all clatter to the ground. And the people reach out to each other and hold hands, with God's voice echoing through them."

There was a silence. The Storyteller nodded, her eyes full of feeling. She remembered that story. It was one of the most important stories she had ever told. And after hearing it from the traveler, there wasn't much more she needed to say.

So she sat, and the travelers gradually resumed their talking. Each story reminded them of another, and they talked and told stories and ate pineapple and hugged and laughed and cried until the sky began to lighten. Then they all lay down and drifted off to sleep as the birds began their morning songs.

The Storyteller looked at them, and she smiled. She stood up, gazing at the sleeping travelers, and murmured, "I am you." And she lay down next to them and fell asleep too.

One World at a Time

One evening, in a forest, a little girl and her grandfather sat next to a campfire. The fire crackled and hissed, a warm breeze blew, and somewhere far off an owl hooted. It was dark and quiet and calm, and the little girl and her grandfather sat gazing into the dancing light of the fire.

The little girl said, "Grandpa, I was thinking. How did all this get to be here? I mean, the trees are so tall and straight, with the branches just right to protect our tent, and the rocks are here for us to put our backpacks on, and the firewood we use smells so great when it burns. It's like it was all set up specially for us, just for us to come out here camping. How did that all happen?"

"Well," said the grandfather, poking a stick into the fire and watching the sparks fly, "I don't know, really."

They sat in silence for a while, and then the girl said, "Grandpa, I was also wondering. Are there animals in the forest? I mean, I know there are squirrels and chipmunks and that funny groundhog we saw today. But are there animals like . . . like bears and stuff? Animals that might want to come and eat us or something? Do you think there are?"

The grandfather thought for a moment. "Oh, probably some," he said, poking the fire again.

More silence. "And Grandpa," she said, "the world seems so strange. I mean, here we are. It's quiet and we just had dinner, but right now, on the other side of the world, it is morning, and people are getting up and going to work. And somewhere else there are people who are eating lunch, and people who are watching movies, and people who are sleeping, and people who are driving cars, and people who are having babies, and people who are laughing, and people who are crying—and it's all happening at once. That is so strange!"

"Sure is," said the grandfather, adding a new log to the fire. "Sure is."

The little girl took a deep breath as she looked up at the blanket of stars shining in the clear and warm night.

"You know what I think about sometimes, Grandpa? I think about what it would be like to get into a spaceship and fly out to the stars. Do you realize that every one of those stars is a sun just like ours, and maybe there are planets around some of them? And if I got into a spaceship and kept going and going, I could fly past one star, and then another, and then a hundred others, and then a million others, and on and on and on. I would keep seeing new and different stars, and I could go on forever, and it would never ever end. That really weirds me out. Forever, and it wouldn't end! Doesn't that really weird you out?"

"Yep," said her grandfather, tilting his head and looking up at the sky. "I suppose it does."

The girl looked back into the fire, feeling its warm glow on her face. And she said, "Grandpa, sometimes I get this funny feeling, like when I'm at school, and someone does something bad, like hitting someone else. I feel like I need to do something

to stop it. If I don't, I get this yucky feeling inside, like I'm not doing the right thing. And when I do help someone, or pick up trash I see on the ground, or something like that, I get this good feeling inside, like I did the right thing. It's kind of like there's a little voice inside me saying what's good to do and what's not good to do. Does that ever happen to you?"

"Oh yeah," said the old man. "All the time."

"And Grandpa, some kids at school say that if we believe in certain things, we'll go to heaven, but if we don't, we'll go to hell. I don't want to go to hell, and I get scared when they say that. I keep thinking about what might happen after I die. What if I don't go to heaven? What if I go to hell?"

The old man was silent.

"I just don't understand," she said, tossing a pine cone into the fire. "It's all so complicated. None of it makes sense."

"Yep," the grandfather said, "you're right." He leaned forward and poked the fire one more time, sending a shower of sparks upward. And then he added, "But you know what I think? I think that I'm here in this forest, and you're here too, and we are together. I don't know why and I don't know how. But I like it—seems like heaven enough for me. And if somehow you got lost or hurt, I can't imagine a worse hell than that. That's what I know. There's no sense worryin' about heavens and hells we don't know. We might as well just live in the ones we do know, right here, right now. One world at a time, that's what I say, one world at a time."

The fire crackled and hissed, and a warm breeze blew. Somewhere far off an owl hooted. It was dark and quiet and calm. Amidst the beauty and the mystery of the forest, the little girl and her grandfather sat and watched the dancing light of the fire, together.

Other Story Books from Skinner House Books

Colleen M. McDonald, ed. *What If Nobody Forgave? And Other Stories*
Nineteen stories bring to life such virtues as compassion, idealism, justice, responsibility and reverence.

Mary Ann Moore. *Hide-and-Seek with God*
Enchanting tales present God in a variety of multicultural, non-sexist ways—as a transcendent mystery, a spiritual force, peace and silence, the mother and father of life, light and darkness and more.

Jeanette Ross. *Telling Our Tales: Stories and Storytelling for All Ages*
Traditional and original tales from around the world. Ross, a seasoned storyteller, examines the power of stories to offer comfort, inspiration, and connection. Includes tips on how to create and tell stories.

Anika Stafford. *Aisha's Moonlit Walk: Stories and Celebrations for the Pagan Year*
Aisha and her modern-day family celebrate the eight pagan holidays over the course of a year.